Woodchuck at Blackberry Road

*Dedicated to my own little chuckling and
all those whistle-pigs who climb trees.*
    —D.L.

*I dedicate this book to mothers everywhere
who protect and teach their children.*
    —A.D.

Text copyright © 1994 C. Drew Lamm.
Book copyright © 1994 Trudy Management Corporation, 165 Water Street, Norwalk, CT 06856
and the Smithsonian Institution, Washington, DC 20560.

Soundprints is a Division of Trudy Management Corporation, Norwalk, Connecticut.

First Edition
10 9 8 7 6 5 4 3 2
Printed in Singapore

Acknowledgements:
   Our very special thanks to Dr. Charles Handley of the department of vertebrate zoology at the
Smithsonian's National Museum of Natural History for his curatorial review.

Library of Congress Cataloging-in-Publication Data

Lamm, C. Drew.

Woodchuck at Blackberry Road / by C. Drew Lamm ;
illustrated by Allen Davis.
       p.   cm.
Summary: A woodchuck hibernates in the winter, gives birth in the spring, and teaches her young
in the summer how to recognize and escape from predators.
     ISBN 1-56899-087-1
1. Woodchuck — Juvenile fiction. [1. Woodchuck — Fiction.]
I. Davis, Allen, ill. II. Title.
     PZ10.3L33235Wo 1994   94-9241
     [E] — dc20   CIP
                                                          AC

Woodchuck at Blackberry Road

by C. Drew Lamm

Illustrated by Allen Davis

Soundprints

Woodchuck waddles around the apple tree by the grey cottage on Blackberry Road. She eats breakfast there. She holds a fruit in her two front paws and nibbles its sweetness.

Then she stretches out to bask in the morning sun. Her whiskers glisten, wet and sticky from the ripe apples.

Every morning is the same. First, Woodchuck peeks over the top of her burrow to sniff the air and scout out danger. Scan and sniff. Twice she has almost met the teeth of a dog. Scan and sniff. All clear.

Then she wambles along the stone wall for a bite of wild daisy, past the lilac hedge where the wild onion grows, across the patch of bitter buttercup, and finally over to the apple tree.

Always the same. As predictable as the postman.

With autumn asters and goldenrod showing in the yard it will
soon be time for her long sleep underground — she will hibernate.
Nose to the ground, she digs a new burrow behind the swing.

Up in the sunlight, she feeds and grows round. Her belly scrapes the ground.

And then one day she squeezes back into her burrow, curls up tight, and says goodnight for months and months and months.

Snowflakes cover the bushes and trees, ponds freeze, children skate, and people celebrate Groundhog Day.

Still the groundhog sleeps.

She sleeps until winter melts into spring.
Woodchuck emerges, blinks and stretches.
She sniffs the air. She gathers spring grasses and
weaves them into a nest.

On April 22nd, a new chuckling is born.
This new Little Whistle-pig snuggles
beside her three new brothers.
Naked and blind, she nestles close
to her mother's soft tummy, drinks
warm milk and falls asleep.

She stays safe in the burrow until she is four weeks old. Finally, fur covers her skin and her legs are strong. She has grown. When she stretches, she bumps her three siblings.

It's time to venture out. Mother checks the horizon and the air for danger. Scan and sniff. All is clear. She urges Little Whistle-pig and the other chucklings out of the dark earthy-brown den and into the light.

Little Whistle-pig squints as she scrambles from dark brown into stunning bright. The air bursts from earth to blue sky and green clover.

Little Whistle-pig climbs to the top of her mother's back and sits up. A mother mountain! Mother Woodchuck turns and nudges Little Whistle-pig with her nose. She rubs her cheek. And then they eat.

17

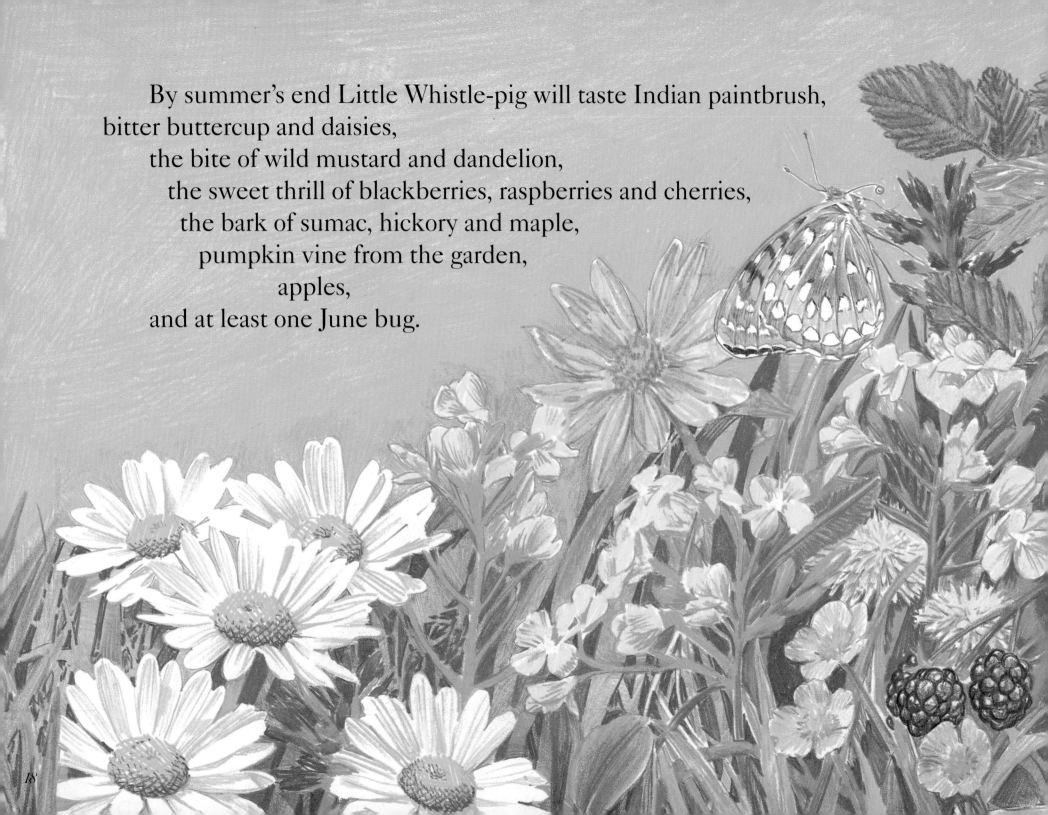

By summer's end Little Whistle-pig will taste Indian paintbrush,
bitter buttercup and daisies,
   the bite of wild mustard and dandelion,
    the sweet thrill of blackberries, raspberries and cherries,
    the bark of sumac, hickory and maple,
    pumpkin vine from the garden,
    apples,
and at least one June bug.

But today, Little Whistle-pig samples the same greens her
mother nibbles and discovers violets.

Mother Woodchuck stops chewing. She sits upright and scans
the landscape — swing, picnic table, and a bicycle on its side.

She smells the air. Violets, clover and phlox. No scent of
predators. No dog or fox. All is clear.

Mother nudges the chucklings, encouraging them to waddle
away from the den. Little Whistle-pig shuffles forward, one, two,
three feet. She buries her nose in the grasses and relaxes.

Suddenly Mother Woodchuck sits upright
again. She scans. She sniffs. She dashes to the den.

Little Whistle-pig and her brothers sit up
scared and confused. Mother grabs Little Whistle-
pig's neck and shovels her home. Her brothers
scramble after them.

The chucklings tumble into their chambers
beneath the yard. But as soon as they are inside the
safety of the den, Mother heads outside again.

Little Whistle-pig follows, uncertainly. Mother Woodchuck moves slowly, sniffing, sniffing, moving her stubby snout back and forth.

Mother trembles. She sits up, peers across the lawn, and bolts to the den.

This time Little Whistle-pig and her brothers scurry right behind.

Inside the safe den, Little Whistle-pig takes great breaths. The earth smells deliciously mossy and dark, full of roots and worms.

Little Whistle-pig shivers. But Mother Woodchuck wags her tail, and it's out into the sunshine again.

The chucklings look around more cautiously now. Two of their cousins, a squirrel and a chipmunk, scurry around the maple tree. All is well. They sniff the air. No danger.

No danger, yet Mother Woodchuck sits
upright and dashes for the den again.
A game!
Little Whistle-pig bolts to the burrow. Her brothers
smack into her as they scramble into the hole.
Mother repeats the dash again and again.
These danger dashes make the breath rush through her.
Some day the danger will be real — a great hairy beast tearing
through the yard with glistening teeth. It would
enjoy a bite of woodchuck.

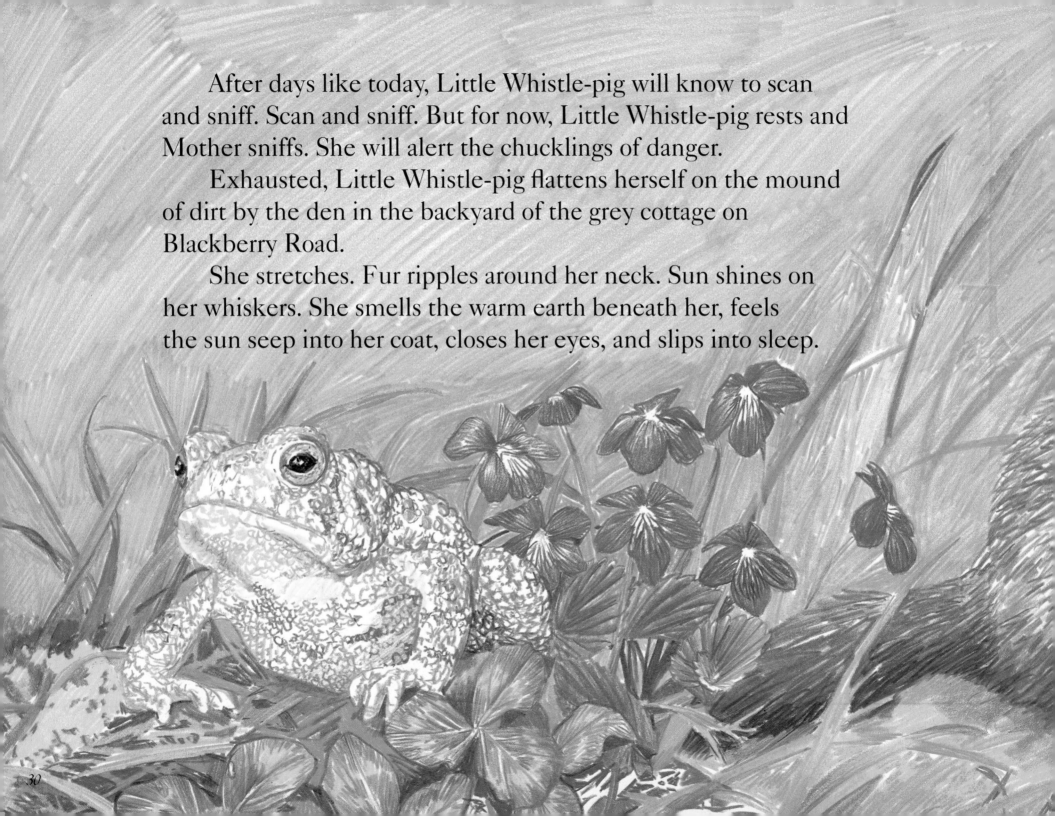

After days like today, Little Whistle-pig will know to scan and sniff. Scan and sniff. But for now, Little Whistle-pig rests and Mother sniffs. She will alert the chucklings of danger.

Exhausted, Little Whistle-pig flattens herself on the mound of dirt by the den in the backyard of the grey cottage on Blackberry Road.

She stretches. Fur ripples around her neck. Sun shines on her whiskers. She smells the warm earth beneath her, feels the sun seep into her coat, closes her eyes, and slips into sleep.

About the Woodchuck

Woodchucks live across Canada and most of the eastern United States. They dig burrows most anywhere, but they prefer pastures and especially open hillsides. Their dens are complex architectural feats made up of chambers, tunnels and numerous entrances. A mound of dirt outside the main entrance is used as a watchtower and place for the woodchuck to bask in the sun. Preferring a clear view of their surroundings, woodchucks are always vigilant for predators, rarely straying far from their safety entrances.

Vegetation, such as grasses and clover, makes up a woodchuck's main diet. Feeding heavily in the autumn, they form thick layers of fat under their skin to sustain themselves through hibernation. In the spring, a litter of four to six chucklings is born. About mid-June, the young disperse, each digging its own den or occupying a vacant one nearby.

Glossary

burrow: A system of underground tunnels and rooms that an animal digs to use as a home.

chuckling: A baby woodchuck.

den: A nest or shelter; in the case of a woodchuck, a burrow.

hibernate: To spend the winter in a state of deep sleep with reduced heart rate, body temperature and breathing.

scan: To slowly look around, particularly for enemies.

sibling: A sister or a brother.

wamble: To waddle unsteadily back and forth.

whistle-pig: Another name for woodchucks, due to the shrill whistling alarm sounds they sometimes make.

Points of Interest in this Book

pp. 4-7, 18-19 buttercups (smallest yellow flower).

pp. 4-5, 16-21, 24-27, 30-31 daisies (white petalled flower).

pp. 4-7, 14-15, 18-21, 26-27, 30-31 dandelions (yellow "pom-pom" flower).

pp. 6-7 lilac bush, praying mantis.

pp. 6-9 goldenrod (yellow fern-like flower), asters (pink flower).

pp. 8-9 box turtle.

pp. 16-17 coneflower (magenta flower).

pp. 16-17, 20-21 black-eyed susans (yellow flower).

pp. 16-17, 20-21, 30-31 clover.

pp. 16-19, 20-21 Indian paintbrush (red flower).

pp. 18-19 wild mustard (yellow petalled flower), blackberries, June bug, fritillary butterfly.

pp. 20-21 phlox (blue flower).

pp. 20-21, 24-25, 30-31 bird's foot violets.

pp. 26-27 sharp-scaly pholiota (mushroom), gray squirrel, eastern chipmunk.

pp. 26-27, 30-31 Anemone blanda (pink flower).

pp. 30-31 American toad.

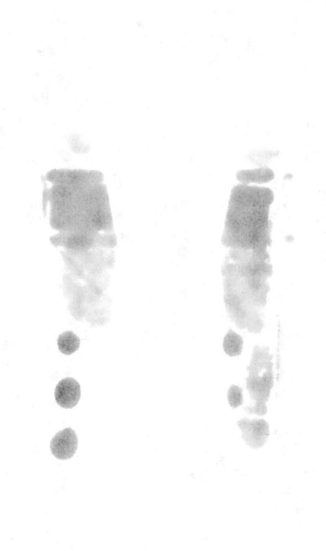

Picture LAMM
Lamm, C. Drew.
Woodchuck at Blackberry Road

4/7/97